Meet Anjali, an inventive little girl with a great big heart. To some, she's a little sassy, but to most, she's clearly clever with much on her mind. But mostly, she's just like everyone else. Except that she's exceptional at the monkey bars. Better than the boys even. Plus, she doesn't yet know that the things you are made fun of for when you are a kid, are exactly what will make you fly when you're all grown up.

Always Anjali

©2018 Sheetal Sheth. All Rights Reserved. No part of this publication may be reproduced, stored in a retrieval system or transmitted in any form by any means electronic, mechanical, or photocopying, recording or otherwise without the permission of the author.

Second Printing, 2019.
Third Printing, 2020.
Fourth Printing, 2021.

Library of Congress Control Number: 2018903132

CPSIA Code: PRT0621D
ISBN-13: 978-1-68401-968-7

Printed in the United States

always Anjali ★

WITHDRAWN

May our littles always feel mighty.

Mad love for my always forever sprites
E.A., M.R., and the mightiest of Mr.'s, N.M.

- S.S.

To all the Anjalis.

With thanks to my family for their
unconditional love and support.

-J.B.

Once upon a restless night, a little girl named Anjali lay wide awake in her bed.

She was turning seven and she had super important business on her mind.

Bikes! All she wanted was one of her own.

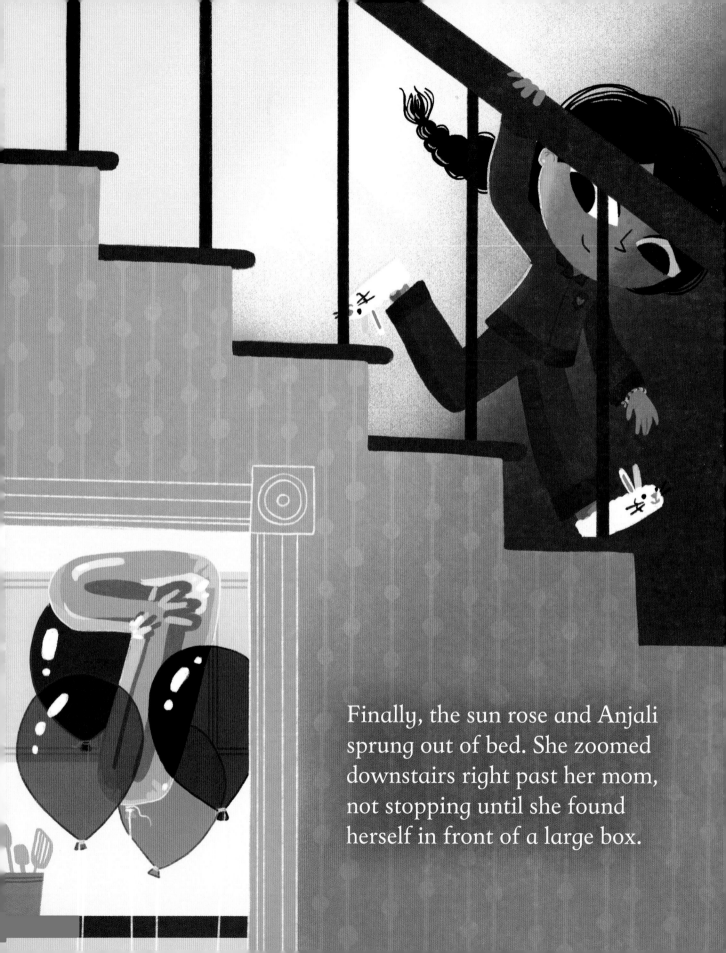

Finally, the sun rose and Anjali sprung out of bed. She zoomed downstairs right past her mom, not stopping until she found herself in front of a large box.

She closed her eyes, took a deep breath, and carefully opened it.

"Thank you, thank you, THANK YOU!

It's perfectly stupendous. Just like a racecar!"
Anjali cheered as she took a spin around the kitchen.

"Can I take it to the school carnival this afternoon?" Anjali hit the brakes at her mom's feet. "Please, please, pretty please?!"

Anjali's face lit up when her mom nodded.

After school, Anjali and her best friends, Mary and Courtney, were riding their bikes together around the carnival.

Mary spotted a booth that was selling personalized license plates. "Awesome! We should all get matching plates for our bikes!"

Anjali and Courtney agreed as they made their way to the booth.

Mary and Courtney found theirs right away.

Anjali looked and looked.

Anjali asked if they had any more plates somewhere else.

"Sorry kid," the cashier grumbled.

"Can you please check?" Anjali pleaded.

The cashier muttered, "What's your name?"

"Anjali."

"Huh? Spell it."

The cashier chuckled and tossed a plate in front of Anjali.

Anjali suddenly heard one of the older boys, Zachary, snickering. "They're not going to have a plate for someone like you, ANN-JELLY!"

Anjali's face got hot.

PEANUT BUTTER AN-JELLY

CAN I GET A PEANUT BUTTER AN-JELLY

WITH A DOT ON TOP?!

Then she heard laughter.

PEANUT BUTTER
AN-JELLY
CAN I GET A PEANUT BUTTER
AN-JELLY?

More classmates had joined Zachary.
Anjali blinked back tears.

At dinner that night, Anjali cleared her throat.
"I am changing my name to Angie," she announced.

"Anjali, why would you want to do that?
Your name is beautiful," Anjali's dad assured her.

"No, it isn't. It's embarrassing! And it's ANGIE!" Anjali cried.

"Your name is a very important part of who you are,"
Anjali's mom said.

"Exactly!" Anjali said defiantly. "And no one has heard of it, no one can spell it, and frankly, I HAAATE IT!"

"You are not changing your name," Anjali's dad said firmly.

"Yes I am, yes I am, **YES I AM!**" Anjali burst into tears and ran to her room.

"Anjali, do you know we picked your name out especially for you? From the moment we saw you, we knew we needed a special name for a special girl. A name whose meaning would capture your spirit."

"My name means something?"
Anjali peeked her head out.

Her mother nodded.

"What? What does it mean?"
Anjali challenged her mom.

"Anjali is a gift. The most precious kind.
Divine. Just like you!"

"Where does it mean that?"
Anjali asked doubtfully.

"In India. It's Sanskrit.

My name, your dad's name, all of
our family's names are from India.

India is an enchanting place,
full of magic, and brilliance, and power."

"Be proud of who you are, Anjali.
To be different is to be marvelous."

"Humph," Anjali mumbled.

Anjali awoke in the middle of the night with a start.

She bolted out of bed with a mission.
She turned on a little lamp and got to work.

An hour later and with the final touches done,
she reviewed her creation one last time.

The next day at school, Mary and Courtney were waiting for Anjali with a box.

Anjali opened the box and to her surprise, she found an ANJALI license plate!

"We made you one exactly like ours!"

"You guys aren't going to believe this but..." Anjali teased gleefully.

She pulled the license plate she had made out of her backpack.

Mary and Courtney squealed.

Their classmates walked over, wondering what was causing all the commotion.

When they saw the special license plate Anjali made, everyone wanted one that would be just as one-of-a-kind!

WOW! YOU MADE THAT?!?
LOVE THOSE COLORS AND HOW YOU DREW THOSE LETTERS.
I'VE NEVER SEEN ANYTHING LIKE IT!
WHAT ARE THOSE BEAUTIFUL LITTLE GEM-LIKE THINGS?
THEY'RE CALLED BINDIS!
COOL! CAN YOU MAKE ONE FOR ME THAT NO ONE WILL HAVE TOO?

After school, when Zachary spotted Anjali, he yelled,

HEY ANN-JELLY!
DID YOU HAVE A PEANUT BUTTER
AN-JELLY SANDWICH FOR LUNCH?

He burst out laughing.

Anjali took a deep breath and stood up straight.
Looking right at Zachary, she quipped, "They're the best kind!"

She hopped on her bike and whizzed past Zachary and his friends.

She had places to go and didn't have time for foolishness.

She knew there was **_greatness_** in not
being one of the crowd.

And vowed to always be Anjali.

Sheetal Sheth, Author

Despite being told she'd have to change her name to work, Sheetal persevered to become an award-winning actress and producer, known for her provocative performances in a wide range of memorable roles on film and television. Sheetal puts a spotlight on under-represented groups, not only through her trailblazing work as an actor, but also by being an outspoken advocate. Sheetal served in President Clinton's AmeriCorps, is on the advisory board of Equality Now, and is an ambassador for The Representation Project. She believes if you can dream it, you can be it - even if you don't see it. Sheetal, her husband, and their two kids live in New York and Los Angeles. This is her first children's book. www.sheetalsheth.com

Jessica Blank, Illustrator

Jessica Blank is an illustrator, explorer, and naturalist living in Texas. She attended the Maryland Institute College of Art and Vermont College of Fine Arts for illustration and graphic design. When not drawing, she enjoys hiking, reading, and spending time with her family. This is her first picture book. www.jessicablank.com

Ashanti Fortson, Additional Art & Background Design

Ashanti Fortson is a Baltimore-based cartoonist and illustrator with a deep love for kind stories and fantastical settings. Their work has been published by The Nib, as well as in various comic anthologies. They write and draw a space fantasy webcomic called "Galanthus," and they hope to one day see the Milky Way. www.ashantifortson.com